Fairy Tale
Twists

For my wonderful Dad.
Thank you for everything
K.D.

For Barney
M.B.

Reading Consultant: Prue Goodwin, Lecturer in literacy and children's books

ORCHARD BOOKS
338 Euston Road, London NW1 3BH
Orchard Books Australia
Level 17/207 Kent Street, Sydney, NSW 2000

First published in 2012
First paperback publication in 2013

ISBN 978 1 40831 210 0 (hardback)
ISBN 978 1 40831 218 6 (paperback)

A CIP catalogue record for this book is available
from the British Library.

1 3 5 7 9 10 8 6 4 2 (hardback)
1 3 5 7 9 10 8 6 4 2 (paperback)

Printed in Great Britain

Orchard Books is a division of Hachette Children's Books,
an Hachette UK company.

www.hachette.co.uk

Fairy Tale
Twists
The Big Bad Werewolf

Written by Katie Dale
Illustrated by Matt Buckingham

ORCHARD

In the middle of a wood
a tiny little cottage stood.
The home of dear, sweet, law-abiding,
kind old little Granny Riding.

Her husband died, her kids have grown,
so now, poor dear, she lives alone.
She still keeps busy – bakes and knits,
she helps the poor, and babysits.

But then one day she looked quite frail.
She dropped her stick, and, turning pale,
she rested for a day or two,
complaining of a nasty flu.

But safe behind her bedroom door,
old Granny did not cough or snore.
Instead, as darkness filled the skies,
she watched the moon begin to rise.
Then quickly – in a blinding **FLASH** –
old Gran began to writhe and thrash!

Her specs fell off, and in a blur
her skin broke out in thick brown fur!
Her dentures tumbled to the floor
as Granny scrambled out the door.
She raised her head and howled with glee.
For Granny was a **WOLF**, you see!

A *werewolf*, to be quite exact,
for months ago she was attacked...
while on her way to see a chum
a stray dog bit her – on the bum!

Since then, each month, for just one night,
she transforms in the full moon's light,
and bounding freely from the wood,
she does things grannies never should!

She crept inside *The Queen of Hearts*
and found a tray of cherry tarts...

She wolfed them down, then ran like mad –
For Gran was big and she was **BAD!**

With impish glee, she switched and swapped,
she took the crumbs that Gretel dropped…

…to throw on Chicken Licken's head!

And filled fruit pies with *birds* instead!

She stole kids' homework, pinched odd socks,
unlocked the door for Goldilocks!
She pushed poor Humpty, chased Bo's flocks,
she even changed the palace clocks!

Then safely tucked in bed at last,
Gran rested till the change had passed.
She grinned, for who would ever guess
a *wrinkly gran* caused all that mess?

She snuggled down and closed her eyes,
when suddenly…

"Hey, Gran – **SURPRISE!**"

"*AARGH!* Who's there?" screamed
   Granny, hiding.

"*Me!*" the girl laughed. "Rose-Red Riding!
I've brought you treats!" Red smiled,
   then stared –

she started getting very scared…

Red knew her Gran was really ill –
sick and full of flu, but still…
she'd not expected such a change.
"Dear Gran," she said, "you're looking
strange…"

"Your ears have grown – how very queer!"

"Better to hear you with, my dear!"

Red stared: "Your eyes are huge!"

  Gran smiled:

"Better to see you with, my child!"

"Your nose has swollen and – good grief!
Dear Gran, what's happened to your *teeth*?"

Gran grinned. "They're truly best of all!
My false teeth were so blunt and small.
I couldn't chew, I couldn't munch.
I'm sick of cabbage soup for lunch!

"But now I'm in for such a treat –
there's *nothing* that I cannot eat!
Oh, how I've longed to gnaw and chew,
and bite and crunch, and eat...

...EAT *CHOO!*"

"Eat *me?*" screamed Red. "Oh help! Oh no!
Is that the time? I've got to go!"

"No, Red – *atchoo!* – come back!"
   cried Gran.
Red fled the house and ran and ran.

She found a woodsman chopping wood.
"Well, hi," he grinned. "I'm Robin Hood."
"Please come!" Red begged. "Fast as you can!
The Big Bad Wolf has eaten Gran!"

Poor Granny jumped out of her bed,
she grabbed her robe and then she fled.

"*There* he is!" the woodsman cried.
"Oh help!" shrieked Gran. "Where *can*
    I hide?"
The grass was thin...

…the rocks were small…

…the trees weren't any help at all!
Their trunks were short,
their branches weak –
so Granny
wound up in
the creek!

The stream was fast, the current strong,
as poor old Gran was swept along...

...towards a wide and very tall,
loud and gushing waterfall!

She splashed about and tried to swim –
then grabbed an overhanging limb.
She scrambled through the slime and muck
to safety, but then – just her luck…

"He's there!" cried Robin. "Come on, Red!"
Poor old Granny filled with dread.
"What now?" she panicked – then she saw
a little cottage made of straw.

"Of course! My friend, the pig!" she cried.
"He'll rescue me – he'll help me hide!"
She raced towards the little hut,
but then – alas! – the door slammed shut!

"Oh, pig!" called Gran. "Please let me in!"
"Oh no! By the hairs on my chinny-chin-chin.
I will not let you in!" the piglet cried.
"As if I'd let a wolf inside!"

"Oh, please!" Gran begged. "I'm old, I'm ill,
it's cold out here – I'll catch a chill!"
Poor Granny coughed, and then she wheezed,
then suddenly poor Granny…

...*SNEEZED!*

She blew straight through the walls of straw –

the house fell flat upon the floor!
Poor Granny stared, quite horrified.

"Oh, HELP! Don't eat me!" Piggy cried.
The piglet fled, with yelps and squeals
with Granny hot upon his heels –
for close behind them, in their tracks
chased Red and Robin – with his axe!

The pig, exhausted by the chase,
soon headed for his brother's place.
Gran raced up to the house of twigs,
and pleaded with the frightened pigs.

"I mean no harm!" poor Granny cried.
"I'm desperate for a place to hide!"
"You can't come in! No chance, no way!"
the piglets cried. "So go away!"

Poor tired Granny huffed and puffed.

"Oh *crumbs*!" cried Piglet One.

 "We're stuffed!"

"He can't get in!" his brother scoffed.

But Granny wheezed and then she…

...COUGHED!

The piglets fled the broken sticks,
and hurried to a house of bricks.
"Oh, not again!" poor Granny groaned.
"I'm far too old for this!" she moaned.

Gran's legs were tired, her fur was wet,
her dressing-gown was drenched in sweat.
"Oh pigs, I beg you – let me in!"
"No, no!" the piglets cried within.

"*You're* the wolf who plays the tricks,
you broke my brother's house of sticks,
and flattened, too, the house of straw –
and now you turn up at *my* door?"

Gran cried, "That wasn't my intent –
the houses were an accident!
I'm not a wolf!" she sighed, confiding –
"I'm really just old Granny Riding!"

The piglets howled. "Yeah, right!" they
  laughed.
"We may be pigs, but we're not daft!"
They rolled around in fits of glee.
"Oh *please*!" Gran wailed. "It's really me!"

Just then: "We've got him!" Robin cried.
"There's nowhere for the wolf to hide!"
Poor Granny looked around in vain,
then scrambled up the piglets' drain!

"You fool!" Rob cried and tossed his cape.
"You're trapped up there – there's no
   escape!"
"It's true!" wailed Gran. "Except… *why not?*"
She tumbled down the chimneypot!

"It's Santa Claus!" one piglet cheered,
as Granny suddenly appeared.
"No, it's the wolf!" his brother cried.
"No, no! It's *Granny*!" Granny sighed.

"Dear pigs, my friends, it's really me!"
"Oh, shame on you!" cried Piglet Three.
"Old Gran would never play such jokes –
the crumbs, the Chicken Licken hoax…
Gran's sweet and kind, for goodness' sake!"
Gran wailed: "All grannies need a break!"

Said Piglet One: "You've got some nerve –
it's time you got what you deserve!"
"Oh no!" cried Gran. "Have mercy, please!
I'm begging you – I'm on my knees!"

Just then, a **FLASH**, a **CRASH** – and then –

old Granny was herself again!

"Well, bless my soul!" cried Piglet Two.
"Old Granny, dear – it's really you!"
Just then, the door burst open wide
and Red and Robin rushed inside.

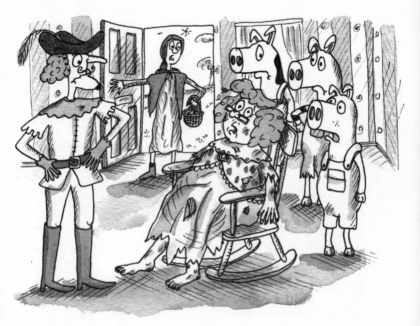

"Stand back!" yelled Robin.

"Gran!" cried Red.

"Thank goodness! I thought you were dead!"

"But where's the wolf?" Rob looked around.

He stared at Gran and then he frowned…

Gran sighed. "The wolf, I must confess…"
"Ran straight through here and wrecked
    Gran's dress!" cried Piglet Two.
"That's right!" said Three.
"He tore her robe and spilt her tea!"

"I'll find him!" Rob raced for the door.
"But *wait* – what do you want him for?
Gran's safe and sound," the third pig said.
"Why don't you stay for tea instead?"

So Rob and Red shared tea and cake,
and laughed about their daft mistake.
"Poor wolf, how awful!" giggled Red.
"But why was he in Granny's bed?"

"He turned up at my house today
And begged me for a place to stay.
He knows now that it wasn't right
To prank and jest and tease all night.
He's learnt his lesson," Granny said,
"and so I tucked him into bed.
He promised me – no more, he's done."

"Hmm," thought Pig One. "Pranks
    sound fun!"

So all lived happily in the end.
Gran did her best to make amends.
Robin fell in love with Red,
and not long after, they were wed.

Yes, all was calm, but then one night,
when the moon was shining bright…
three shadows scurried round in glee!
Now, can you guess who they could be…?

And next time when you see *your* Gran,
watch her closely, if you can.
Look past the smiles and snowy hair –
is something naughty twinkling there?

For just like little Granny Riding,

who knows what secrets *she's* been hiding…?

Fairy Tale Twists

Written by Katie Dale
Illustrated by Matt Buckingham

All priced at £8.99

Orchard Books are available from all good bookshops,
or can be ordered from our website, www.orchardbooks.co.uk,
or telephone 01235 827702, or fax 01235 827703.